Kylie
the Carnival
Fairy

For the fairy fantastic
Magna Sundstrom

Special thanks to
Narinder Dhami

ORCHARD BOOKS
338 Euston Road, London NW1 3BH
Orchard Books Australia
Hachette Children's Books
Level 17/207 Kent Street, Sydney, NSW 2000
A Paperback Original

First published in 2006 by Orchard Books

HiT entertainment

Illustrations © Georgie Ripper 2006

A CIP catalogue record for this book is available
from the British Library.

ISBN 978 1 84616 175 9

14
Printed in Great Britain

Orchard Books is a division of Hachette Children's Books,
an Hachette UK company.

www.hachette.co.uk

Kylie
the Carnival
Fairy

by Daisy Meadows

illustrated by Georgie Ripper

ORCHARD BOOKS

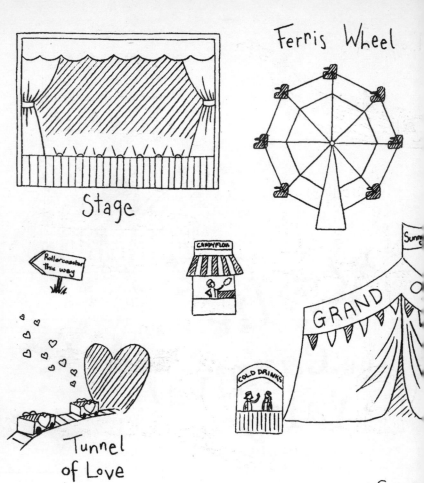

Stage

Ferris Wheel

Rollercoaster
This way

CANDYFLOSS

COLD DRINKS

GRAND

Summ

Tunnel
of Love

Hall of Mirrors

Spinn

Fancy Dress Tent

Log Falls

Hoopla

Carousel

Hook-a-Duck

Ghost Train

Dodgems

Carnival Hat
Hijinks

Fairy magic means carnival fun
While the magic hats are where they belong.
But my icy spells will cause a stir
When those hats are no longer where they were!

Band Leader's hat and Carnival Crown
Both will go missing when I come to town.
But I'll start with the Carnival Master's hat
And send my goblin servants to capture that!

Contents

The Carnival Begins

"This is exciting!" Rachel Walker exclaimed to her best friend, Kirsty Tate. "I've never been to a carnival before."

"Sunnydays is the best carnival of them all," Kirsty replied. "It visits Wetherbury every year at the end of the summer holidays. I'm so glad you're staying with us, so that you can come too."

The girls were standing with Kirsty's parents and a large crowd of people outside the gates of the carnival showground. There was a buzz of excited chatter as everyone waited for the Grand Opening.

"Which ride will you go on first, girls?" asked Mr Tate.

"I don't know," Kirsty said, peering through the gates. "There are so many!" She could see a Ferris wheel, dodgems, spinning teacups and many more. There were also stalls offering sweets and games like hoopla and hook-a-duck.

"Look, Kirsty!" Rachel nudged her friend as a man in a red coat and a black top hat appeared behind the gates.

"He must be the Carnival Master," Kirsty explained. "It's time for the Grand Opening!"

The crowd cheered loudly.

"Ladies and gentlemen," boomed the Carnival Master. "Welcome to Sunnydays, the most magical carnival in the world!" And he threw open the gates with a flourish. "Follow me!"

Rachel and Kirsty hurried inside the showground eagerly, along with the rest of the crowd.

"Let the carnival magic begin!" announced the Carnival Master, sweeping off his top hat and pointing it at the Ferris wheel. Immediately the great wheel began to turn. The crowd gasped.

Then the Carnival Master waved his hat at the teacups, which began to spin in a blur of bright colours.

"It is magic!" gasped a little girl near Kirsty, as the rides sprang to life.

Rachel and Kirsty smiled. They knew all about magic. The two girls had become friends with the fairies, and helped their tiny friends whenever cold, spiteful Jack Frost and his goblin servants were causing trouble.

A loud drumbeat echoed through the air.

"It's the parade!" Kirsty cried.

There was a clash of cymbals and a band, led by a man in a smart blue uniform, marched towards the crowd. The Band Leader wore a blue peaked cap, trimmed with gold braid, and carried a rainbow-coloured baton. As the spectators cheered, he tipped his hat to them and twirled his baton. Immediately, the band struck up a merry tune.

"This is great," Rachel said as the band marched past. "Look, there are dancers and acrobats."

Behind the band came dancers in blue and gold dresses, with long satin ribbons in their hands which they twirled and twisted as they danced.

Acrobats jumped and tumbled, handing out party poppers in between cartwheels. Kirsty and Rachel were delighted to get one each.

"There are jugglers too!" Kirsty pointed out.

The jugglers wore red and white jester's hats with bells on, and carried colourful juggling balls.

"Oh, dear!" Rachel sighed as one of the jugglers dropped all his balls at once. "I think they need a bit more practice."

Kirsty frowned as another of the jugglers stumbled into one of the acrobats. "They're not very tall, are they?" she said. "Perhaps they're children. That would explain why they're not very good at juggling yet." But then Kirsty glanced down at the jugglers' feet. Their shoes were huge – much too big for children's shoes!

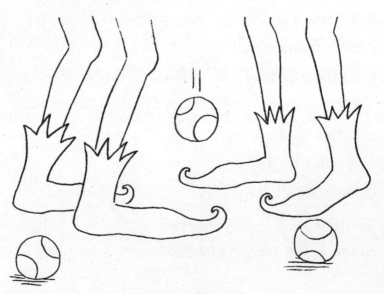

Kirsty peered closely at the jugglers as they paraded past. Although their hats hid most of their faces, she could just make out that they had long, green noses.

"Rachel!" Kirsty whispered, her heart pounding. "Those jugglers aren't children. They're goblins!"

Goblins Make Mischief

"Oh, no!" Rachel gasped, realising Kirsty was right.

"Why are Jack Frost's goblins here?" Kirsty wondered, counting them quickly. "Rachel, there are eight of them!"

"And Jack Frost has made them bigger too," Rachel added.

"They're almost as tall as us. That must be so that they don't stand out in the crowd."

"I bet they're up to no good!" Kirsty said, frowning.

"Now, let me present our most magical ride," the Carnival Master was saying.

"Look at the goblins," Kirsty whispered.

All eight goblins were dashing straight towards the Carnival Master. As they got close to him, the biggest goblin suddenly jumped up  and knocked the top hat off his head!

The Carnival Master cried out in surprise, but everyone else laughed, thinking it was part of the show. One of the other goblins caught the hat as it fell, and then they all disappeared into the crowd.

"Why do the goblins want the Carnival Master's hat?" Kirsty asked, as the shocked Carnival Master struggled to continue with his announcement.

"Er, as I was saying," he stammered. "This is the most important ride of the carnival!" He pointed at a huge green and gold sheet, which was clearly screening something very large.

Two clowns on stilts stood either side of the sheet, each holding a corner. There was a drum roll from the band, and then the clowns pulled the sheet away to reveal a brightly-painted carousel of elegant, high-stepping horses – but unlike the other rides, this one didn't start turning.

"The carousel will be working soon," the Carnival Master said hastily. "Meanwhile, please enjoy our other wonderful rides!"

But as Kirsty and Rachel looked around the showground, they saw that the Ferris wheel seemed to be stopping, and the teacups were slowing to a halt too.

Suddenly, out of the corner of her eye, Kirsty caught a flash of red and white.

It was the goblins again. And this
time they were rushing towards the
Band Leader.

"Look out!" Kirsty cried, trying to
warn him.

But the band was playing too loudly
for him to hear. Once again the tallest
goblin jumped up and knocked the hat
off the Band Leader's head. Another

goblin swept it up off the ground, and all the goblins raced away.

The instant the Band Leader lost his hat, he also lost control of the band. The tubas and flutes sounded out of time, the trumpeters started marching in the wrong direction and the drummers dropped their drumsticks. The tuneful music became a deafening din.

"Why are the goblins trying to spoil the carnival?" Rachel wondered.

"I don't know," Kirsty sighed.

The band had stopped playing now, and the Band Leader was looking dazed. The Carnival Master rushed forwards. "Don't forget," he announced, "for the Closing Day Parade, we want you all to come in fancy dress. The boy or girl with the best costume will be crowned Carnival King or Queen with our splendid Carnival Crown!"

Just then Rachel and Kirsty heard the clip-clop of hooves behind them. Everyone turned to see two women in sparkly pink costumes riding white ponies.

The women carried a blue velvet cushion between them, and on top of the cushion sat the Carnival Crown, studded with gems and feathers.

"And now I declare Sunnydays Carnival officially open!" the Carnival Master cried proudly.

The crowd cheered and scattered to explore the carnival.

"We must find out what the goblins are up to," Rachel said anxiously.

Kirsty nodded, beginning to shiver.

"It's suddenly got cold, hasn't it?" she said, her teeth chattering.

Rachel nodded and rubbed her arms. "It's been warm all day until now," she said, frowning.

At that moment Kirsty noticed a clown in a baggy yellow costume and curly green wig standing nearby. He was staring intently at the Carnival Crown.

Kirsty nudged Rachel. "Look," she whispered. "There's something familiar about that clown."

Rachel stared at the clown. Then, with a start, she noticed frosty icicles hanging from his chin. "Kirsty," Rachel gasped. "That's Jack Frost!"

Kylie Pops In

Kirsty stared at Jack Frost in horror. "He's used his magic to make himself as big as the goblins," she whispered to Rachel.

At that moment, the goblins suddenly reappeared. Trying to juggle, they quickly surrounded the Carnival Crown.

Meanwhile Jack Frost had conjured up an icy wind which swept him up and carried him through the air. Only Kirsty and Rachel noticed as he zoomed towards the crown; everybody else was too busy watching the goblin jugglers.

The girls stared in dismay as Jack Frost snatched the crown from its cushion and zoomed away out of sight. Immediately, the goblins gathered up  their juggling balls and hurried after him. Rachel and Kirsty tried to follow, but the goblins disappeared too quickly.

"The crown!"
gasped one of
the women on
the ponies.
"Where did it go?"

"Maybe it fell off
the cushion," the
other suggested, and
they began looking
around for it.

"Now Jack Frost has the Carnival
Master's hat, the Band Leader's hat
and the Carnival Crown!" Kirsty said
anxiously. "What's he going to do
with them?"

"Let's go and see," Rachel suggested.

Kirsty turned to her parents, who
were chatting to some friends. "Mum,
can Rachel and I go on the rides?"

Mrs Tate nodded. "We'll meet you at the gates in half an hour," she replied. The girls hurried after the goblins.

Suddenly, Rachel felt a tingling in her fingers. She glanced down to see that she was still holding her party popper. And now it seemed to be shaking all by itself!

Suddenly the party popper exploded in a shower of glitter. Rachel jumped as streamers shot into the air. "Oh!" she said in surprise.

A fairy was hovering amid the streamers, beaming at the girls. As the streamers floated to the ground, the fairy flew to Kirsty's shoulder.

Her skirt, striped in all the colours of the rainbow, billowed around her as she landed.

"Hello, girls!" the fairy called, pushing a few strands of her dark brown hair out of her eyes. "I'm Kylie the Carnival Fairy!"

"Hello," Rachel gasped.

"As Carnival Fairy, it's my job to make sure the Sunnydays Carnival is a huge success," Kylie explained. "But Jack Frost is trying to ruin everything!"

"Why?" asked Kirsty.

"Because he got bored in his ice castle," Kylie sighed. "And so he's decided to spoil everybody's fun."

"What about the hats?" Rachel wanted to know.

Kylie winked at the girls. "The hats are magic!" she said with a grin. "The Carnival Master's hat makes sure all the rides run smoothly."

"No wonder the carousel wasn't working," Kirsty gasped.

Kylie nodded. "The magic of the Band Leader's hat makes the carnival music perfect," she went on. "That's why the band can't play in tune anymore. And the Carnival Crown makes sure that Sunnydays Carnival ends happily and can move on to the next town."

"So if we can't get the hats back, the carnival will be ruined for everyone!" Rachel cried.

"We can't let that happen," Kirsty added.

"I knew you'd help me, girls," Kylie declared happily. "Now, where are Jack Frost and his goblins?"

"They went that way," Rachel said.

As the girls looked in that direction, Kirsty spotted a flash of red and white.

"There's a goblin," she said excitedly, pointing him out to Rachel and Kylie. "And he's got the Carnival Master's hat!"

Goblins Go for a Ride

"After him!" Kylie cried, sliding into Rachel's pocket out of sight.

The girls hurried towards the goblin, but before they could reach him, he spotted them.

"It's those pesky girls!" he shouted to his two companions. "Quick, hide!"

The three goblins immediately dashed off, closely followed by the girls.

As the goblins passed the ghost train, one of them skidded to a halt. "In here!" he shouted. Ignoring the 'Broken — Please Come Back Later' sign, the three goblins rushed inside.

Kirsty and Rachel blinked as they saw a shimmer of magic and suddenly, all the lights outside the ghost train came on.

BROKEN
- Please
Come Back
Later

"The magic of the Carnival Master's hat is making the ride work," Kylie explained.

The giggling goblins climbed into the front carriage of the train, and Rachel and Kirsty just managed to jump into the carriage behind as the train pulled away.

As the train turned the corner, the girls saw spiders' webs and bats hanging from dark trees. A cold wind howled around them.

Rachel and Kirsty knew it was only
a sound effect, but the goblins had
stopped giggling and were muttering
to each other in scared voices.

"Whoooooooo!" a ghost jumped out
from behind a tree, moaning loudly.
The goblins shrieked with fright.

"I don't think the goblins are enjoying
the ride!" Kirsty laughed.

As the train rattled round another corner, a loud creaking sound filled the air.

"What's that?" the goblins wailed. Then they screamed in terror as a coffin swung open, and a vampire with long sharp fangs leaned out to grab them.

Eventually, the train shot through the doors and came to a stop. Still moaning with fright, the goblins leapt out of the train and ran away.

"They're heading for the Log Falls ride," Kylie said. "Quick!"

The Log Falls ride wasn't working. It had a 'No Entry' sign outside. But, once again, the goblins ignored the sign and jumped into one of the floating, log-shaped boats. Immediately, there was a dazzling flash of magic.

"The Carnival Master's hat's at work again," Rachel said.

Sure enough, water was beginning to tumble and splash along the waterways, and the goblins' little boat floated away.

Kirsty turned to Rachel and Kylie. "What are we going to do?" she asked.

Rachel was staring at the waterways. "I've got an idea!" she announced.

Goblins Outwitted!

"What is it?" Kylie asked eagerly.

"Look!" Rachel pointed at the ride. At the bottom of one of the waterways was a long slide.

"The goblins will be coming down that slide soon," Rachel explained. "If we stand at the bottom, we can try to grab the hat as they go past."

"Perfect!" Kylie exclaimed.

The goblins were out of
sight on one of the other
waterways, but the
girls and Kylie
could hear them
squealing with
delight. Quickly
they hurried over
to the bottom
of the slide
and waited.

"They're at
the top of the slide,"
Rachel whispered, as
the goblins' boat floated
into sight. "Get ready!"

At that moment, the log boat
tipped over the edge and shot down

the slide towards the girls.
"Yee-hah!" the goblins
yelled, waving their arms
in the air. They were
sitting one behind the
other in the little
boat. Rachel, Kirsty
and Kylie could see
that the goblin
with the Carnival
Master's hat was
right at the back.
The boat zoomed
down to the bottom of
the slide. Kirsty was
closest to the waterway, and
as the boat splashed past, she
reached out and snatched the hat right
out of the astonished goblin's grasp!

"Give that back!" the goblin yelled furiously as he was carried past. "Stop the boat!" But there was nothing the goblins could do. The boat swept on along the waterways, taking the angry goblins with it.

"Well done!" laughed Kylie, as Kirsty shook drops of water off the hat. "Now, let's take it back to where it belongs."

Kylie slipped into
Rachel's pocket
again, and they
all hurried off to
the main tent,
a huge white marquee
in the middle of the showground. The
Carnival Master was standing in the
entrance with the Band Leader, looking
very unhappy.

"I think we might have to close
the carnival," the Carnival Master was
saying. "Too many rides
aren't working!"

"We're just in time," Kirsty
whispered.

"But how are we going to give the
hat back?" Rachel asked. "They'll want
to know where we found it!"

"Kylie, could you make us fairy-sized?" Kirsty asked quietly. "And the hat too? Then we'll be able to return it without being seen."

Kylie nodded. Quickly the girls slipped behind the tent, where Kylie waved her wand over them. Rachel, Kirsty and the hat immediately shrank to fairy-size. Then, carrying the tiny hat, the girls and Kylie flew back to the tent entrance.

They waited until the Carnival Master went to check on the rides, then they flew inside and put the hat on his desk. Immediately, Kylie waved her wand again and the hat shot back to its usual size.

Then they fluttered back outside, and Kylie's magic soon turned Rachel and Kirsty into normal girls again.

A moment later, they heard the Carnival Master returning to the tent.

"We'll have to close down," he said to the Band Leader. "I'll make an announcement."

Kirsty, Rachel and Kylie peeped
round the side of the tent as the
Carnival Master went inside.
"My hat!" he exclaimed
in surprise. "How
did that get there?"
And he picked it
up and put it on.
Rachel and
Kirsty beamed
at each other as
suddenly, all around them,
they heard the whirr and purr of rides
starting up again. The Ferris wheel was
moving, the teacups started spinning
and the dodgems were soon bumping
into each other.

"Look, even the carousel's turning!"
Rachel pointed out.

"Everything's working again!" the Band Leader exclaimed in amazement.

"That's wonderful!" the Carnival Master gasped, rushing out of the tent to see. "It's almost like magic!"

Kylie laughed as she turned to Rachel and Kirsty. "It *is* magic, girls!" she said. "And I couldn't have got the magic hat back without you." She smiled at them. "Now I must be off to Fairyland to tell everyone the good news."

"We'd better go and find my mum and dad," Kirsty said.

Rachel nodded. "But we'll be back tomorrow to help you find the other hats," she promised Kylie.

"Thank you, girls," Kylie called, waving as she disappeared in a dazzling shower of sparkles.

"What a meanie Jack Frost is," said Kirsty, as she and Rachel headed for the gates. "He hates to see people having fun."

"Well, we won't let him spoil the carnival!" Rachel said in a determined voice. "I wonder if we'll find another hat tomorrow?"

Musical Muddle

Contents

Mirror Magic

"I'm glad Mum and Dad let us come to Sunnydays Carnival early today," Kirsty remarked, as she and Rachel walked round the carnival ground. It was the second day of the carnival and it was sunny again with clear blue skies.
"It gives us more time to look for the magic hats."

"Well, you did tell them we wanted to go on all the rides!" Rachel said with a grin.

"Yes, but Dad says we must meet up later so that we can all go on the roller coaster together," laughed Kirsty. "That's his favourite."

Suddenly, a terrible din made Rachel clap her hands over her ears. "What's that noise?" she cried. "It's horrible!"

"It's the band," Kirsty said sadly. "No wonder it sounds awful — they don't have the magic of the Band Leader's hat to make sure all the music goes smoothly!"

"Look!" Rachel pointed at the stage. "The dancers are putting on a show. That's why the band's playing."

The girls walked towards the stage, but as they got closer, they saw that nothing was going right. Not only was the band playing out of tune, but it was out of time too. The dancers couldn't keep in step, so they kept bumping into each other.

"The Band Leader looks very upset," whispered Kirsty.

Rachel saw that the Band Leader was conducting the music, and wincing at every wrong note. Only a few people were watching the show, and some of them had their fingers in their ears.

Just then, the Carnival Master hurried onto the stage, looking flustered. "Thank you, dancers," he said loudly, "The show's over, ladies and gentlemen!" And he began to clap.

A few members of the audience clapped too, but rather half-heartedly, as they began to move away.

The Carnival Master shook his head in despair. "I don't know what's going on," he said, staring at the dancers. "You're usually so good!" He sighed. "Come along, you need a break. I'll take you to the refreshments tent for tea and biscuits."

Looking glum, the dancers trailed off the stage.

"I think you'd better go too," the Band Leader said, looking sadly at his musicians. "We'll try again later."

"The music won't sound right till we get the Band Leader's hat back," Kirsty said as she and Rachel watched the gloomy musicians put down their instruments and leave.

"Maybe we should start looking for it right away," Rachel suggested. "I bet the goblins are still around here somewhere, enjoying the carnival."

"Oh, but remember what the fairies always say," Kirsty grinned at her. "We must let the magic come to us!"

Rachel laughed. "In that case, why don't we have some carnival fun ourselves?" she said.

"Good idea," Kirsty agreed.

The girls wandered round the showground, enjoying the sunshine. They passed a fancy dress and face-painting tent, and a man selling candyfloss. Next door was the hall of mirrors.

CANDYFLOSS

HALL of

Fancy Dress

"Oh, I love this!" Rachel said eagerly. "Let's go in."

Kirsty swung the door open, and the girls stepped inside. For a split-second it was dark, but as the door closed, the lights came on. Immediately the girls were surrounded by hundreds of Kirstys and Rachels, reflected in the tall mirrors all around them!

"This is weird," Rachel laughed, turning this way and that. Her reflections turned this way and that too. "Look, Kirsty," She raised her arms, and hundreds of

Rachels raised their arms too. Before Kirsty could speak, there was a sudden pop, and a burst of multi-coloured glitter suddenly appeared in mid-air and surrounded the girls as it floated to the ground. "Where did that come from?" Kirsty gasped in surprise and delight. The glitter was reflected in all the mirrors, making the girls feel as if they were surrounded by dazzling fireworks.

"Look," Rachel cried, "Fairies!"

There, dancing in the mirrors, the girls could see hundreds of tiny fairies, their wings fluttering and shimmering with light. It was such a magical sight

that Kirsty and Rachel could hardly believe their eyes!

Then Rachel laughed. "Oh, look, it's not hundreds of fairies," she told Kirsty. "It's Kylie!"

Suspicious Scouts

"Hello girls!" called a silvery voice behind them, and the girls turned to see Kylie smiling happily. "I'm so glad to see you," she went on. "I can sense that the Band Leader's hat isn't far away!"

"Great!" Kirsty said eagerly. "Let's keep our eyes open."

"First we have to find the way out of here," said Rachel, looking around in confusion at all the mirrors.

"The exit door must have a mirror on the back to hide it," Kirsty said with a frown.

"I'll help," Kylie said, smiling and waving her wand. A shower of magic pink sparkles flew from the wand and surrounded one of the mirrors in a glittering frame of fairy dust.

Rachel hurried over and pushed the mirror. It swung open, and as the girls made their way outside, Kylie flew down to Kirsty's shoulder and hid behind her hair.

Kirsty and Rachel stood outside the hall of mirrors looking around. Rachel turned and saw the fancy dress tent. A group of cub scouts in their dark green uniforms were gathered just inside, squealing with delight as they tried on different outfits and had their faces painted.

Rachel was about to turn away, when she suddenly realised that something wasn't quite right. For one thing, there were no carnival people at the tent – the boy scouts were painting each other's faces! Rachel stared a little harder.

"Look at those scouts," she said
to Kirsty and Kylie.

Kirsty and the little fairy turned to
look. At that moment, one of the
scouts, who was dressed as a witch,
rushed forwards and
pushed another, who
was still in his
scout uniform but
had an orange
and black
stripy tiger's
face, out of the
face-painting chair.

"It's my turn now!"
yelled the first scout, sitting
down and whipping off his witch's hat.
Now Kylie, Rachel and Kirsty could all
see that his face was green!

"He's a goblin!" Rachel breathed.

"They're all goblins!" Kirsty added.

The girls edged closer to the tent.
They could see that the goblins had
been very busy. One was dressed in
a monkey suit, with a monkey mask.
And another was wearing a black suit
with white bones on it so that he
looked like a skeleton! Rachel noticed
that his face had been scarily painted in
black and white to look like a skull.

"Look at the one doing the painting!"

Kirsty whispered to
Rachel and Kylie.
They couldn't help
laughing when they
saw that the goblin
looked exactly like
Jack Frost! He wore
a cloak round his shoulders and had
a spiky wig and beard which he had
clearly painted white to look
like Jack Frost's icy hair.

He was glaring at
the witch goblin who
had sat down to have
his face painted. "You
don't need painting!" he
snapped. "Everybody knows
witches are supposed to be green."

Suddenly, through the open doorway of the tent, Rachel spotted the Band Leader's blue and gold hat on the table. "There's the hat!" she whispered excitedly, pointing it out.

"Girls, if I make you fairy-sized, perhaps we can slip in and get the hat back without being spotted," Kylie whispered.

Rachel and Kirsty nodded, Kylie waved her wand, and soon the girls were tiny fairies with glittering wings on their backs. Then all three friends flew cautiously towards the fancy dress tent.

Frightening Faces

Just before the friends reached the
entrance, the tiger-faced goblin
hurried over to the table. To the
girls' dismay, he grabbed the Band
Leader's hat and jammed it firmly
on his head. Then he marched out
of the tent.

"After him!" whispered Kirsty.

The tiger-faced goblin started to hurry off across the showground.

"Where are you going?" the skeleton goblin shouted after him.

The goblin stuck his tongue out. "I'm going to have some fun on the rides!" he yelled. He looked very silly in his scout uniform, with his tiger's face, the Band Leader's hat perched on his head, and his tongue sticking out! Rachel, Kylie and Kirsty couldn't help laughing.

"I want to have fun too!" roared the skeleton goblin, dropping the pirate costume he'd been about to try on.

"So do we!" shouted the other goblins, throwing down the paint tubes and bits of costumes they were holding.

"Let's go!" Rachel whispered. And the three friends flew after the goblins, wondering which ride they would head for.

But the tiger-faced goblin stopped
when he saw the 'Hall of Mirrors' sign.
"What's a hall of mirrors?" he asked.

"Oh, you are silly!" scoffed the goblin
in the monkey suit. "Everyone knows
what a hall of mirrors is!"

"Well, what is it?" asked the first goblin.

"It's…er…" The monkey-faced goblin's voice trailed away and he looked very uncomfortable.

"He doesn't know!" scoffed the wicked witch goblin. "Let's go inside and find out!" He pulled open the door and the goblins began fighting to get in first.

"We'll slip inside before they close the door," Kylie whispered to the girls. "One, two, three, go!"

As the door swung
shut, Kylie, Rachel
and Kirsty
swooped forwards
and managed
to dart inside.

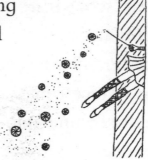

Just as before, the lights came on as
soon as the door closed. Hovering high
overhead, Rachel,
Kirsty and Kylie
could see the
goblins' painted
faces reflected
hundreds of
times in the
mirrors. The
goblins could see
them too, and they
stared at the mirrors in alarm.

"Help!" shrieked the tiger-faced goblin. "Where have all these scary monsters come from?"

"Get me out of here!" roared the Jack Frost goblin. "I can see hundreds of tigers!"

"Uh-oh, Jack Frost's here — dozens of him!" the monkey-faced goblin yelled in terror. "And he looks really angry!"

Foiled Again

Kirsty turned to Kylie and Rachel. "The goblins don't realise they're looking at their own reflections," she laughed. "They're scaring themselves silly!"

"I can see skeletons!" moaned the wicked witch goblin. "Hundreds of horrible skeletons come to life!"

He backed away from the mirrors and cannoned straight into the tiger-faced goblin. They bumped into each other so hard that the Band Leader's hat fell off.

Suddenly the tiger-faced goblin gave a shout. "Hey! Those monsters aren't monsters!" he gasped. "They're us!" And he pointed at the mirror nearest him.

"The tiger's pointing at us!" gasped the monkey-suited goblin in terror.

"That's because it's ME!" the tiger-faced goblin shouted impatiently. "It's my reflection!"

Kirsty was laughing so hard she thought she would burst, and Kylie was giggling too.

But Rachel was staring at the hat lying on the floor. "Now's our chance," she whispered. "Together we can lift it!"

Kylie and Kirsty stopped laughing and nodded as the goblins stared more closely at the mirrors and finally realised what the tiger-faced goblin had been telling them.

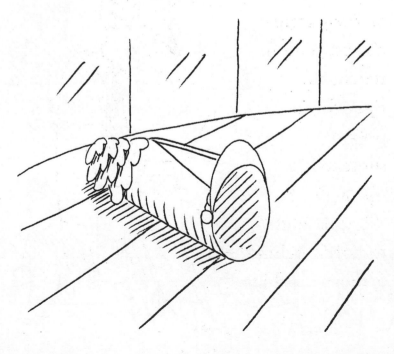

"I knew it all along!" said the Jack Frost goblin. "What a lot of silly fools you are!"

"Who are you calling a fool?" snapped the tiger-faced goblin.

Rachel, Kirsty and Kylie fluttered down over the goblins' heads towards the hat, but just as they were almost within reach, the tiger-faced goblin snatched it up! Kylie and the girls had to zoom behind a mirror to hide.

"I've found the door!" yelled the wicked witch goblin, suddenly, pushing it open. The goblins tumbled out into the sunshine, still arguing loudly, and the door slammed shut behind them. This time Kylie and the girls weren't quick enough to fly out.

"We nearly had the hat that time!" Rachel sighed.

"We mustn't give up," Kirsty said firmly. "Kylie, can you make us human-sized again so we can open the door?"

Kylie nodded and in a shower of magic sparkles from her wand, the girls shot up to their normal size. Then they raced out of the Hall of Mirrors with Kylie perched on Rachel's shoulder.

"There go the goblins!" Rachel said, pointing ahead.

"It looks like they're heading for the teacups," added Kirsty.

The girls hurried after them. The carnival was even busier now than it had been earlier, and all the rides the girls passed were full, including the carousel. Rachel smiled to see children sitting on the pretty wooden horses, beaming happily as they whizzed round and round. But then she frowned. "The carousel music sounds awfully tinny and out of tune!" she remarked.

"So does the music on the dodgems," Kirsty agreed, as they hurried on past the bumper cars.

"Music is very important in making sure everyone enjoys the carnival," Kylie sighed. "That's why we must get the Band Leader's hat back soon!"

Giddy Goblins!

The goblins were looking excited as they headed for a large pink teacup. They all climbed in and waited for the ride to start.

"What now?" asked Rachel, staring at the tiger-faced goblin who was still wearing the magic hat.

Kirsty had been thinking hard.

"I've got an idea," she said slowly, as the ride started up. "Kylie, could you make the teacup spin even faster than usual?"

Kylie's eyes twinkled. "Oh, yes," she replied. The goblins were enjoying themselves as the ride turned and their teacup began to spin. Smiling, Kylie pointed her wand at the goblins' cup and sent sparkling fairy dust rushing towards it. The teacup began to spin faster.

"Hurrah!" shouted the goblins. "This is fun!"

"That's not fast enough!" Kylie laughed, and she waved her wand again.

Now the teacup began to whizz round even more quickly. Rachel and Kirsty could see that the goblins were starting to look woozy and even greener than usual! The teacup was now moving so fast that the tiger-faced goblin was forced to hang on to the side. Kylie raised her wand one last time, and a shower of sparkles made the teacup spin super-fast, so that the goblins were almost a blur. The witch's hat was on tightly, but the Band Leader's hat wasn't. The tiger-faced goblin put up a hand to hold the Band Leader's hat on, but he was too late.

It flew off his head and went
spinning through the air.
"My hat!" the tiger-faced
goblin shrieked.
"Stop the teacup!"
moaned the wicked
witch goblin, "I want
to get off!"

Rachel hurried over and picked up the
hat, as Kylie lifted her
wand to slow the
teacup down again.
Then the girls
watched as the ride
stopped and the
goblins climbed off.
They were so dizzy that
they couldn't walk straight. Rachel
giggled as they bumped into each other.

"Thank goodness we've got the hat back," said Kylie. "But now we must take it to the Band Leader. It's almost time for the afternoon show."

They hurried off to the tent next to the stage. The Band Leader was standing outside with the Carnival Master, and as the girls and Kylie approached, they could hear them talking.

"It's time for the show," the Carnival Master was saying. "Look, there are lots of people in the audience and the dancers and the band have had a break now. I'm sure they'll be much better."

The Band Leader nodded, but he
looked rather doubtful as he went into
the tent where his musicians were
tuning their instruments. Rachel, Kirsty
and Kylie followed. They peeped
through the tent flap and saw the band
lining up with the dancers behind them.

"How are we going to give the hat back?" Rachel whispered.

"The Band Leader hasn't picked up his baton yet," Kirsty said, noticing it on the table. "Kylie, maybe you could make the hat appear right next to it?"

Kylie winked. With a flick of her wand she made the hat shrink. Then she sent the tiny hat whizzing through the tent flap and over to the table. It landed neatly next to the baton. With a final wave of her wand, Kylie made it grow back to its normal size.

115

"Perfect!" Kirsty beamed.

The Band Leader hurried over to the table to pick up his baton, but he stopped in surprise as he saw his hat lying next to it. "My hat!" he gasped. "How did that get there?" Smiling from ear to ear, the Band Leader put his hat on, picked his baton up and cleared his throat. "Now, let's try and play a bit better than earlier, shall we?" he said to the band.

Looking rather nervous, the Band
Leader took his place at the head of
the parade and raised his baton. The
trumpeters played a fanfare as they
all marched towards the tent opening.
Rachel, Kirsty and Kylie drew back,
to watch the parade.

The band broke into a lively tune, played in perfect time, and the girls grinned at each other. On stage, the dancers twirled their batons and performed their steps expertly, never missing a beat. The audience began to applaud loudly.

"Everything is back to normal!" Rachel said with a sigh of relief, turning to glance at the carousel. The horses were still spinning, and the music sounded sweet and tuneful now.

"Not quite everything!" Kylie replied. "The goblins still have the Carnival Crown. And without that, the carnival won't be able to move on to the next town, which means lots of other boys and girls will miss out!"

"Don't worry, Kylie," Kirsty said. "We'll do our best to find the crown."

Kylie smiled gratefully. "Thank you,"

she said. "But it's your carnival too!
So go and enjoy yourselves now, while
I return to Fairyland and tell the King
and Queen the latest news. They'll be
so pleased to hear we've only one
magic hat left to find!" She waved her
wand in farewell. "See you tomorrow."

Rachel and Kirsty waved as Kylie
disappeared in a shower of sparkles.

"It's time to meet Mum and Dad at the roller coaster," said Kirsty.

"Well, Kylie did tell us to go and enjoy ourselves," Rachel replied with a grin. "And tomorrow, we'll be on the look-out for the Carnival Crown!"

Carnival
Crown

Contents

Cats and Clowns

"I can't believe it's the last day of the carnival!" Kirsty said, slipping on her eye mask. "How do I look, Rachel?"

"Brilliant!" Rachel laughed.

Both girls were wearing their fancy dress costumes, ready for the closing day parade.

The parade and a fireworks display were taking place that evening, but the girls had visited the carnival earlier in the day, hoping to find the missing Carnival Crown. Unfortunately, they hadn't seen a single goblin or any sign of the stolen crown.

Rachel and Kirsty were dressed as black cats in black trousers, black jumpers and black velvet eye masks. Mrs Tate had made them a fluffy tail each, and the girls had drawn whiskers on their faces with black eyeliner.

"Pearl doesn't look impressed!" Kirsty laughed, glancing at her cat who was snoozing on her bed.

Rachel smiled, then frowned nervously. "I'm looking forward to the parade, but I'm worried," she said. "If we don't find the crown, Sunnydays Carnival won't be able to finish properly and move on to the next town."

Kirsty nodded. "Let's hope we have some luck tonight," she said.

"Are you ready, girls?" Mr Tate called.

"Coming!" Kirsty yelled, as she and Rachel hurried downstairs.

Kirsty's parents were dressed up as clowns with baggy suits and red noses. They both clapped admiringly when they saw the girls in their costumes.

"You look lovely," said Mrs Tate.

"So do you!" laughed Kirsty.

"Just don't trip over your tails," Mr Tate added as they all set off.

The carnival was in full swing when they arrived. Dusk was falling, and all the stalls were brightly lit. The weather had turned icy cold, but there were still long queues of people waiting for every ride. Rachel and Kirsty were glad that their costumes were cosy.

"It's not going to be easy to spot the goblins in this crowd!" Rachel whispered.

"We'll just have to keep our eyes open," Kirsty replied. "Oh, look, Rachel – hook-a-duck!" She pointed at the stall where little yellow, plastic ducks were bobbing in a tub of water. "Let's have a go."

"We're going to get a cup of tea," said Mrs Tate. "We'll meet you at the

fireworks display later, OK, girls?"
Kirsty and Rachel nodded and hurried over to the hook-a-duck stall as Mr and Mrs Tate headed off across the showground.

Kirsty paid the stallholder, and he handed each of the girls a fishing-rod with a hook on the line, so that they could try and catch the ducks.

Rachel concentrated on the duck floating nearest to her. It bobbed away a few times, but at last she managed to catch it. As she pulled it towards her, she heard a tiny voice cry, "Hello, Rachel!"

Rachel was so surprised she almost dropped the duck!
Then she looked more closely and saw Kylie perched neatly on the duck's back.

Rachel grinned and nudged Kirsty. "I've hooked something better than a duck," she laughed. "Look!"

Quickly the girls put down their fishing-rods and the duck, and moved away from the stall with Kylie.

"Jack Frost is here!" Kylie said breathlessly, fluttering onto Rachel's shoulder. "He thinks his goblins haven't been causing enough mayhem at the carnival, so he's come to keep an eye on them, and he's got the Carnival Crown!"

"That's why it's so cold tonight!" exclaimed Kirsty, and Kylie nodded.

"Have you seen any goblins, Kylie?" Rachel asked. But no sooner were the words out of her mouth, than she saw three small figures in jester hats hurrying towards the tunnel of love.

"Look!" Rachel gasped, as she spotted their green faces. "Goblins!"

Finding Jack Frost

"Well spotted, Rachel," said Kylie.

"Let's follow them," Kirsty suggested.

The three goblins jumped into the front car of the train standing outside the tunnel of love. Rachel, Kirsty and Kylie quickly climbed into another carriage a little further back.

The train slowly set off into the
tunnel. Inside it was quite dark, so the
girls took off their masks and stuffed
them in their pockets.

They soon saw that the tunnel of love
was based around the four seasons.
First they travelled through the spring
section, where there were pretty pictures
of gardens full of daffodils and bluebells.

Summer came next, and the scenes showed a park with people picnicking and sunbathing. Here the air felt warmer and a park bench stood under a pretty pergola of roses. In the autumn section it became cooler again, and there were model trees with leaves of red, orange and gold.

The winter scene was the last one and the coldest. Here, there was fake snow on the ground and pictures of people ice-skating and sledging. Models of snowmen and frosty trees were dotted here and there.

The train slowed down as it reached a curve in the track, and the girls were surprised to see the goblins leap off and disappear behind one of the painted scenes.

"Quick!" whispered Rachel. "We'd better follow!"

The girls stepped down from their carriage and hurried to hide behind a plastic tree.

"Hurry up, you idiots!" bellowed a voice from the shadows, making Kylie and the girls jump. They peeped out from their tree to see Jack Frost sitting on a throne of ice!

"He's wearing the Carnival Crown!" whispered Kirsty, excitedly. Jack Frost glared at his goblins. "You're having too much fun!" he snapped. "You should be spoiling the carnival for the humans, not enjoying it yourselves!"

"Maybe we can creep along behind the scenery, sneak up to the throne and grab the crown right off his head!" Rachel suggested.

"Good idea," Kylie agreed. So Rachel and Kirsty began to edge carefully towards the throne.

"WELL?" Jack Frost roared.

"I've got an idea for ruining the carnival," one goblin volunteered. "We could steal all the toffee-apples and eat them!"

"We can frighten little children!" another shouted.

"And we could put wet paint on the saddles of all the carousel horses!" suggested another goblin eagerly.

"Excellent!" Jack Frost declared, rubbing his hands gleefully. "And I'll keep the Carnival Crown here, so that those pesky fairies can't get their hands on it!"

The goblins cheered. Then, giggling nastily, they all ran back out to the carnival, just as Rachel and Kirsty reached the throne. The girls could see the crown poking above the back of it.

"Can you reach it, Rachel?" Kylie whispered.

"I'll try," Rachel replied, cautiously stretching out her hand. But suddenly the crown was whisked away as Jack Frost leapt to his feet. The girls jumped, and Kylie almost fell off Rachel's shoulder.

"Thought you could fool me, did you?" Jack Frost sneered, peering round the throne at them. "Well you can't! I knew you were there all the time!"

"We want the crown, please!" Rachel cried.

"Yes, you must give it back!" Kirsty added bravely.

But Jack Frost only laughed, pointed his wand at the girls and fired two ice bolts straight at them.

Ice Lightning

Just in time, Rachel and Kirsty
managed to jump out of the way
before the lightning bolts struck. When
they peeped out again, Jack Frost had
jumped into the last car of another
train. As it disappeared around the
corner, he gave the girls and Kylie
a cheery wave.

"After him!" cried Kirsty, and the girls rushed out of the tunnel of love.

As soon as they were back in the showground, they realised that the goblins had already started spoiling everything.

"A jester stole my toffee-apple!"
sobbed one little boy, while a little girl
was complaining that her dress was
covered in paint. As
Kylie and the girls
wondered what to
do next, they saw
a goblin jester pop
out from behind
a tree and shout
BOO! at a little girl
who burst into tears.

"The goblins are being
horrible!" Kirsty said, frowning.

Rachel nodded. "We need to get the
Carnival Crown back," she said firmly.

"It won't be easy," Kylie pointed out.
"Everyone's in fancy dress, so Jack Frost
will be hard to spot."

Suddenly there was a loud BANG. "Oh!" Rachel exclaimed in surprise. She glanced up and saw a trail of silver sparks across the sky. "Surely it can't be time for the fireworks yet?" she murmured.

"That's no firework," Kylie cried. "It's one of Jack Frost's ice bolts!"

"It came from over there," Kirsty said, pointing towards the Log Falls ride.

Quickly, the girls dashed towards the ride. Sure enough, there was Jack Frost, and he was using his magic to freeze all the water in the Log Falls waterways.

"Oh, no," Kirsty sighed. "He's found a new way to spoil the carnival!"

Looking very smug, Jack Frost marched off. Rachel, Kylie and Kirsty followed.

"I bet he's looking for another ride to freeze!" said Rachel.

But Jack Frost joined the queue for the Ferris wheel. He stared up at it, his eyes shining.

"He can't freeze that, can he?"
Kirsty asked.

"I don't know," Kylie replied,
sounding worried. "Let's join the queue
behind him. And, girls, put your masks
back on so Jack Frost
won't recognise you."

Rachel and Kirsty
slipped their masks on
and joined the queue.

"Just one little ride," Jack
Frost was muttering to himself.
"I've always wanted to go on a Ferris
wheel. And the goblins will never
know!" He looked around guiltily, to
make sure no goblins were watching.
Kirsty and Rachel's hearts pounded as
he glanced past them, but he didn't
recognise them behind their masks.

"He's going on the Ferris wheel!"
Rachel whispered.

"We'll go too!" Kirsty replied.

Looking excited, Jack Frost climbed
into a car. Immediately the girls and
Kylie jumped into the next one, and the
Ferris wheel began to turn.

Rachel glanced upwards. Jack Frost's car was above theirs as they were lifted into the air. But Rachel realised that once they got past the highest point and started to move back down, Jack Frost would be below them. *If only we had something to hook the crown with,* Rachel thought, *we could lift it straight off Jack Frost's head!*

Suddenly, Rachel spotted the hook-a-duck stall. "I've got an idea!" she exclaimed. "Kylie, could you magic a fishing rod with a big hook at the end of the line — like the ones for hook-a-duck?"

"Oh!" Kirsty looked excited. "You mean, we can hook-a-crown!"

"No problem," Kylie laughed. She fluttered into the air and waved her wand. With a flash of sparkles, a shiny gold fishing-rod appeared in Rachel's hands. "We're going over the top of the wheel," Kirsty announced. "Now we're above Jack Frost."

Rachel took off her mask and leaned forwards, trying to catch the Carnival Crown below her with the hook on the end of her fishing line. She came close, but the wind kept blowing the hook the wrong way. But Kylie fluttered down, gently caught the hook and attached it to the crown.

Hardly daring to breathe, Rachel began to lift the crown off Jack Frost's head...

A Queen is Crowned

Jack Frost didn't notice a thing as Rachel drew the crown upwards. He was having too much fun enjoying the ride!

"Well done, Rachel," Kirsty whispered as she freed the crown from the fishing line.

Kylie beamed at the girls.

"Now we can make sure the carnival ends happily," she said. "We'll be just in time for the crowning ceremony!"

All the rides were coming to a halt now. The parade had started and soon it would be time for the Carnival King or Queen to be crowned. As soon as the Ferris wheel stopped, the girls jumped out of their car. Rachel glanced nervously at Jack Frost, but he still hadn't noticed that the crown had gone.

But just then a goblin hurried up to him. "The crown!" he shouted, pointing at Jack Frost's head. "Where's it gone?"

Jack Frost clapped his hands to his head and immediately realised that the crown wasn't there. Furiously he spun round and his icy glare met Rachel's. Her heart sinking, Rachel remembered that she hadn't put her mask back on.

"You again!" Jack Frost shouted.
Then he spotted the crown in Kirsty's
hands. "I want that crown!"

"Run!" shouted Kylie.

The girls took to their heels,
Kylie clinging to Kirsty's shoulder.
They headed for the main stage, where
the crowning ceremony was due to
take place. Jack Frost raced after them.

"The Carnival Master's on stage,"
Rachel panted. "We're almost there!"

But at the same time, the girls could hear Jack Frost chanting a spell behind them. "Don't think you can escape from me. These balls will stop you, wait and see!" he cried.

As the girls passed the coconut shy, a bucket of balls overturned and the balls rolled and bounced across the grass, right under the girls' feet. Rachel slipped and Kirsty stumbled. The crown flew out of Kirsty's hands and sailed through the air towards the stage.

"Oh, no!" Rachel cried as she saw Jack Frost racing after it.

Jack Frost caught the crown at the

edge of the stage, just as the Carnival Master stepped up to make an announcement. "I'm afraid the Carnival Crown has gone missing," he said sadly. "But the Carnival King or Queen will still receive free tickets to next year's carnival."

But as the Carnival Master spoke, a spotlight came on and lit up Jack Frost in a blaze of white light. He stood there, blinking, crown in hand.

"The Carnival Crown!" gasped the
Carnival Master, hurrying over to Jack
Frost. "You've found it! That's
wonderful!" The crowd applauded
wildly as the Carnival Master shook
Jack Frost warmly by the hand.
"And what a fantastic costume!"
he added admiringly.

Rachel, Kirsty and Kylie watched as Jack Frost was drawn on stage by the Carnival Master in a storm of applause.

"Look, Jack Frost is blushing!" Kylie whispered.

And it was true! Jack Frost was clearly enjoying all the attention. He had a very smug look on his face.

"Please help me announce the winner," said the Carnival Master, and Jack Frost looked even more pleased.

Rachel nudged Kirsty as she noticed the goblins cheering at the front of the crowd.

The Carnival Master held up a piece of paper, and Jack Frost read out: "Our Carnival Queen this year is Alexandra Kirby, for her beautiful princess costume!"

A little blonde girl in a pretty princess outfit walked on stage smiling. The Carnival Master helped her  to sit on the golden throne and then turned to Jack Frost for the crown.

Jack Frost frowned, and clung to the crown as the Carnival Master tried to take it. But, eventually, he had to let go. He couldn't do anything else in front of such a large audience.

As the Carnival Queen was crowned, he stomped sulkily off stage. But immediately a crowd of children surrounded him.

"Please can I have your autograph?" asked one little boy.

"How did you find the crown?" asked another.

"Can we take your photo?" begged two little girls.

Looking flustered, Jack Frost tried to move away, but the children followed.

"Jack Frost has a fan club!" Kylie remarked, laughing, as she and the girls headed away from the stage. "Girls, how can I ever thank you? Now Sunnydays Carnival can move on for other children to enjoy."

"We were glad to help!" Rachel smiled.

"And it must be nearly time for the fireworks," added Kirsty. "We'd better go and find Mum and Dad."

As she spoke, a huge, glittering cloud of fairy dust exploded in the air ahead of them.

"Look, Kirsty!" Rachel gasped, as the dust began to clear. In front of them the carousel was spinning and sparkling with fairy magic. And there, on a painted unicorn's back, sat King Oberon and Queen Titania.

Very Special Guests

"What are you doing here?" Rachel asked, looking delighted as the King and Queen flew over to her.

"We've only ever seen you in Fairyland before," said Kirsty.

King Oberon smiled. "We've come to thank you for all your help," he said.

"Thanks to you, Sunnydays Carnival is saved!" added the Queen.

"What about Jack Frost?" Kirsty asked anxiously.

"Don't worry about him!" The King said, pointing at Jack Frost who was happily signing autographs for all the children. "He's enjoying himself."

"Jack Frost loves to be the centre of attention," the Queen explained. "While he's so popular, he won't cause any trouble for Sunnydays."

"Come here!" Jack Frost was telling his goblins. "Collect up these autograph books and carnival programmes. I'll sign them all!"

Rachel and Kirsty laughed.

"So the carnival's safe at last!" said Rachel.

"Yes, and these are to say thank you," Queen Titania replied. She lifted her wand and touched first Kirsty's hand, then Rachel's. Suddenly each girl found herself holding a tiny, glittering model of a carousel!

"Look, Rachel," Kirsty gasped in delight. "They're exactly the same as the Sunnydays carousel!"

"And the horses move round too!" Rachel added, turning her carousel. "They're beautiful!"

A whooshing noise made them all look up, just in time to see a shower of red and green sparks light up the sky.

"The fireworks display is starting," said King Oberon. "You'd better hurry back to Kirsty's parents, girls.

Kylie, the Queen and I have work
to do!"

The Queen smiled and winked at

Rachel and Kirsty.
"We have to make
sure the fireworks
are extra-special
this year!" she
laughed. And Kylie
clapped her hands in joy.

"Goodbye!" cried Rachel and Kirsty.
"And thank you for our beautiful gifts."

The fairies waved their wands, and
then zoomed into the night sky in
a shower of rainbow-coloured sparkles.
Seconds later, as the girls joined Kirsty's
parents, the sky was filled with a mass
of fireworks glittering in all the colours
of the rainbow.

"Goodness me!" gasped the Carnival Master, looking surprised. "I don't remember buying such fabulous fireworks!"

Rachel and Kirsty grinned at each other. They were the only ones who knew that there was a little royal fairy magic adding a lot of extra sparkle to the Sunnydays Carnival.

Now Rachel and Kirsty must
help...

Megan the Monday Fairy

Read on for a sneak peek...

"I'm glad I'm staying with you for half-term," Kirsty Tate told her friend, Rachel Walker, as they came out of Fashion Fun, the accessories shop on Tippington High Street. "And I hope these sparkly clips will look nice with my new hairstyle!"

"I'm sure they will," Rachel said cheerfully. "They're so pretty."

"Thanks," Kirsty replied. "I wonder how the fairies are," she added, lowering her voice.

Rachel and Kirsty shared a magical secret: when they had first met on a very special holiday to Rainspell Island, they had become friends with the fairies!

"I hope Jack Frost and his goblins are behaving themselves," Rachel said.

Cold, spiteful Jack Frost and his mean goblin servants often caused trouble for the fairies, and the girls had helped their tiny friends outwit Jack Frost many times.

"Look, Rachel!" Kirsty said, peering into a nearby window. "This shop wasn't open last time I was here. Isn't it lovely?"

The shop was called Dancing Days, and the window was full of dance costumes and dancing shoes. There were white tutus with gauzy net skirts, satin ballet slippers with pink ribbons and sparkly tap shoes.

"I'd love to be able to tap dance," said Rachel.

Just then the shop door opened and a lady emerged, followed by a girl with long brown hair in a ponytail.

The girl's face lit up when she saw Rachel.

"Hi, Rachel!" she called.

"Hi, Karen," said Rachel with a smile. "Kirsty, this is Karen. She's a friend from school. And this is her mum."

Karen grinned at Kirsty. "It's nice to meet you," she said. "Rachel talks about you all the time!"

Kirsty laughed. "Are you learning to dance?" she asked, glancing at Karen's blue bag.

"Yes," Karen replied. "I've got my tap class at the town hall this afternoon and Mum's just bought me some new tap shoes. My old ones were worn out."

"That's because she practises so much!" Mrs Lewis said, smiling. She glanced at her watch. "We'd better hurry, Karen."

"See you later!" Karen called as they left.

"Maybe you could sign up for Karen's tap classes," Kirsty suggested to Rachel as they walked down the street.

"Good idea," Rachel agreed. "Shall we walk home through the park?"

"OK," Kirsty replied.

The girls walked through the iron gates and across the grass. The borders were bright with colourful flowers, and in the middle of the garden was a large brass sundial shining in the sun.

"The sun's bright today," Kirsty said. Rachel nodded. Then she noticed something that made her heart beat faster: tiny golden sparkles were hovering and dancing above the sundial!

"Kirsty, look at the sundial!" Rachel gasped. "I think it's fairy magic!"

Kirsty's eyes widened. Rachel was right. And now the golden sparkles were moving. As the girls watched, the fairy dust drifted down to circle around a tiny door in the base of the sundial.

Rachel frowned. "I've seen this sundial hundreds of times, but I've never noticed a door before," she said.

Suddenly the little door burst open and a frog hopped out. He wore a smart red waistcoat and a gold pocket watch. "Hello, Rachel. Hello, Kirsty," he croaked.

The girls beamed at him. "You must be from Fairyland!" Rachel guessed.

The frog nodded. "I'm Francis, the Royal Time Guard," he explained. "I'm a friend of Bertram's." The girls had met Bertram, the frog footman, during their fairy adventures.

"Is everything OK?" Kirsty asked.

Francis shook his head, looking sad. "The King and Queen of Fairyland need your help!" he croaked. "Will you come?"

"Yes, of course!" Rachel and Kirsty chorused.

"Thank you, girls," Francis beamed. He reached into his pocket and pulled out some fairy dust which he threw into the air. Immediately a dazzling rainbow, shimmering with colour, began to rise up from the ground.

"Follow me," said Francis, hopping into the end of the rainbow.

Rachel and Kirsty both stepped carefully into the rainbow beside Francis. "Now off we go!" he said with a smile, and, in a shower of sparkles, the rainbow whizzed them all away to Fairyland.

Read Megan the Monday Fairy to find out what adventures are in store for Kirsty and Rachel!

Meet the fairies, play games
and get sneak peeks at
the latest books!

www.rainbowmagicbooks.co.uk

There's fairy fun for everyone at
www.rainbowmagicbooks.co.uk.
You'll find great activities, competitions, stories and
fairy profiles, and also a special newsletter.

Win Rainbow Magic Goodies!

There are lots of Rainbow Magic fairies, and we want to know which one is your favourite! Send us a picture of her and tell us in thirty words why she is your favourite and why you like Rainbow Magic books. Each month we will put the entries into a draw and select one winner to receive a Rainbow Magic Sparkly T-shirt and Goody Bag!

Send your entry on a postcard to Rainbow Magic Competition, Orchard Books, 338 Euston Road, London NW1 3BH. Australian readers should email: childrens.books@hachette.com.au New Zealand readers should write to Rainbow Magic Competition, 4 Whetu Place, Mairangi Bay, Auckland NZ. Don't forget to include your name and address. Only one entry per child.

Good luck!

Summer fun with the fairies

Look out for the fabulous Rainbow Magic specials.
Each one features three new adventures for
Kirsty, Rachel and a special fairy friend!

Meet the
Fun Day Fairies

Collect them all to find out how Kirsty and
Rachel save the Fairyland Fun Day Flags
from Jack Frost and his goblins!

www.rainbowmagicbooks.co.uk

Enjoy special days with the fairies!

Look out for the fabulous Rainbow Magic specials.
Each one features three new adventures for
Kirsty, Rachel and a special fairy friend!

Christmas fun with the fairies!

Look out for the fabulous Rainbow Magic specials.
Each one features three new adventures for
Kirsty, Rachel and a special fairy friend!